Charles Swain

Dryburgh Abbey and other poems

Charles Swain

Dryburgh Abbey and other poems

ISBN/EAN: 9783337206284

Printed in Europe, USA, Canada, Australia, Japan

Cover: Foto ©Andreas Hilbeck / pixelio.de

More available books at **www.hansebooks.com**

DRYBURGH ABBEY

AND

OTHER POEMS.

DRYBURGH ABBEY

AND

OTHER POEMS.

BY

CHARLES SWAIN,

AUTHOR OF "THE MIND," "DRAMATIC CHAPTERS," "ENGLISH MELODIES," ETC.

London: Simpkin, Marshall, & Co., Paternoster Row.

Manchester: A. Ireland & Co., Pall Mall.

1868.

TO

ARCHIBALD WINTERBOTTOM, ESQ,

THIS VOLUME IS INSCRIBED,

WITH

SINCERE APPRECIATION AND AFFECTION.

MEN are agents for the future !
  As they work, so ages win
Either harvest of advancement,
  Or the product of their sin !
Follow out true cultivation—
  Widen education's plan :
From the majesty of nature
  Teach the majesty of man !
Take the spade of perseverance :
  Dig the field of progress wide :
Every bar to true instruction
  Harrow out and cast aside !

Give the stream of education
  Broader channel, bolder force :
Hurl the stones of persecution
  Out, where'er they block its course :
Seek for strength in self-exertion : .
  Work and still have faith to wait :
Close the crooked gate to fortune :
  Make the road to honour *straight !*
Take the spade of perseverance :
  Dig the field of progress wide :
Every bar to true instruction
  Harrow out and cast aside !

CONTENTS.

Contents.

DRYBURGH ABBEY.

'TWAS morn—but not the ray which falls the
    summer boughs among,
  When beauty walks in gladness forth, with all
    her light and song ;
'Twas morn—but mist and cloud hung deep upon the
  lonely vale,
And shadows, like the wings of death, were out upon
  the gale.

For He whose spirit woke the dust of nations into
  life—
That o'er the waste and barren earth spread flowers
  and fruitage rife—
Whose genius, like the sun, illumed the mighty realms
  of mind—
Had fled for ever from the fame, love, friendship of
  mankind !

B

To wear a wreath in glory wrought his spirit swept
    afar,
Beyond the soaring wing of thought, the light of
    moon or star ;
To drink immortal waters, free from every taint of
    earth—
To breathe before the shrine of life, the source whence
    worlds had birth !

There was wailing on the early breeze, and darkness
    in the sky,
When, with sable plume, and cloak, and pall, a
    funeral train swept by ;
Methought—St. Mary shield us well!—that other
    forms moved there,
Than those of mortal brotherhood, the noble, young,
    and fair !

Was it a dream ?—how oft, in sleep, we ask, "Can
    this be true ?"
Whilst warm Imagination paints her marvels to our
    view ;—
Earth's glory seems a tarnished crown to that which
    we behold,
When dreams enchant our sight with things whose
    meanest garb is gold !

Was it a dream ?—methought the "dauntless Harold"
    passed me by—
The proud "Fitz-James," with martial step, and dark
    intrepid eye ;

That " Marmion's" haughty crest was there, a mourner
  for his sake ;
And she,—the bold, the beautiful !—sweet " Lady of
  the Lake."

The " Minstrel " whose *last lay* was o'er, whose
  broken harp lay low,
And with him glorious " Waverley," with glance and
  step of wo ;
And " Stuart's " voice rose there, as when, 'mid fate's
  disastrous war,
He led the wild, ambitious, proud, and brave " Vich
  Ian Vohr."

Next, marvelling at his sable suit, the " Dominie "
  stalk'd past,
With " Bertram," " Julia," by his side, whose tears
  were flowing fast ;
" Guy Mannering," too, moved there, o'erpowered by
  that afflicting sight ;
And " Merrilies," as when she wept on Ellangowan's
  height.

Solemn and grave, " Monkbarns" appeared, amidst
  that burial line ;
And " Ochiltree " leant o'er his staff, and mourned
  for "Auld lang syne !"
Slow march'd the gallant "Mc. Intyre," whilst "Lovel"
  mused alone ;
For *once*, " Miss Wardour's " image left that bosom's
  faithful throne.

With coronach, and arms reversed, forth came " Mac
    Gregor's " clan—
Red "Dougal's" cry peal'd shrill and wild—" Rob
    Roy's" bold brow look'd wan :
The fair " Diana " kissed her cross, and bless'd its
    sainted ray ;
And "Wae is me" the "Baillie" sighed, "that I
    should see this day !"

Next rode, in melancholy guise, with sombre vest
    and scarf,
Sir Edward, Laird of Ellieslaw, the far-renowned
    " Black Dwarf;"
Upon his left, in bonnet blue, and white locks flowing
    free—
The pious sculptor of the grave—stood " Old Mor-
    tality !"

"Balfour of Burley," " Claverhouse," the "Lord of
    Evandale,"
And stately " Lady Margaret," whose wo might
    nought avail !
Fierce " Bothwell" on his charger black, as from the
    conflict won ;
And pale " Habakkuk Mucklewrath," who cried
    " God's will be done !"

And like a rose, a young white rose, that blooms mid
    wildest scenes,
Passed she,—the modest, eloquent and virtuous
    " Jeanie Deans;"

And " Dumbiedikes," that silent laird, with love too
deep to *smile,*
And " Effie," with her noble friend, the good " Duke
of Argyle."

With lofty brow, and bearing high, dark " Ravens-
wood" advanced,
Who on the false " Lord Keeper's" mien with eye
indignant glanced :—
Whilst graceful as a lonely fawn, 'neath covert close
and sure,
Approached the beauty of all hearts—the " Bride of
Lammermoor !"

Then "Annot Lyle," the fairy queen of light and
song, stepped near,
The " Knight of Ardenvhor," and *he,* the gifted
Hieland Seer ;
" Dalgetty," " Duncan," " Lord Monteith," and
" Ranald," met my view ;
The hapless "Children of the Mist," and bold
" Mhich-Connel Dhu !"

On swept " Bois-Guilbert"—" Front de Bœuf"—" De
Bracy's" plume of wo ;
And " Cœur de Lion's" crest shone near the valiant
" Ivanhoe ;"
While soft as glides a summer cloud " Rowena" closer
drew,
With beautiful " Rebecca," peerless daughter of the
Jew !

Still onward like the gathering night advanced that
    funeral train—
Like billows when the tempest sweeps across the
    shadowy main ;
Where'er the eager gaze might reach, in noble ranks
    were seen
Dark plume, and glittering mail and crest, and wo-
    man's beauteous mien !

A sound thrill'd through that length'ning host !
    methought the vault was clos'd,
Where, in his glory and renown, fair Scotia's bard
    reposed !
A sound thrill'd through that length'ning host ! and
    forth my vision fled !
But, ah !—that mournful dream proved true,—the
    immortal Scott was dead !

The vision and the voice are o'er ! their influence
    waned away
Like music o'er a summer lake at the golden close of
    day :
The vision and the voice are o'er !—but when will be
    forgot
The buried Genius of Romance—the imperishable
    Scott ?

The Angel-watch.

THE ANGEL-WATCH, or THE SISTERS.

A DAUGHTER watched at midnight
   Her dying mother's bed;
  For five long nights she had not slept,
   And many tears were shed:
A vision like an angel came,
  Which none but her might see;
" Sleep, duteous child." the angel said,
  " And I will watch for thee !"

Sweet slumber like a blessing fell
  Upon the daughter's face ;
The angel smiled, and touched her not,
  But gently took her place;
And oh, so full of *human* love
  Those pitying eyes did shine,
The angel-guest half mortal seemed—
  The slumberer half divine.

Like rays of light the sleeper's locks
  In warm loose curls were thrown ;
Like rays of light the angel's hair
  Seemed like the sleeper's own.

A rose-like shadow on the cheek,
   Dissolving into pearl;
A something in that angel's face
   Seemed *sister* to the girl!

The mortal and immortal each
   Reflecting each were seen;
The earthly and the spiritual
   With death's pale face between.
O human love, what strength like thine?
   From thee those prayers arise
Which entering into Paradise,
   Draw angels from the skies.

The dawn looked through the casement cold—
   A wintry dawn of gloom,
And sadder showed the curtained bed,—
   The still and sickly room:
" My daughter?—art thou there my child?
   Oh, haste thee, love, come nigh,
That I may see once more thy face,
   And bless thee, ere I die!

If ever I were harsh to thee,
   Forgive me now," she cried;
" God knows my heart, I loved the most
   When most I seemed to chide;

Now bend and kiss thy mother's lips,
  And for her spirit pray !"
The angel kissed her; and her soul
  Passed blissfully away !

A sudden start !—what dream, what sound,
  The slumbering girl alarms ?
She wakes—she sees her mother dead
  Within the angel's arms !
She wakes—she springs with wild embrace—
  But nothing there appears
Except her mother's sweet dead face—
  Her own convulsive tears.

WHAT IS NOBLE ?

WHAT is noble ?—to inherit
    Wealth, estate, and proud degree ?—
      There must be some other merit
        Higher yet than these for me !—
Something greater far must enter
  Into life's majestic span,
Fitted to create and centre
  True nobility in man.

What is noble ?—'tis the finer
  Portion of our mind and heart,
Link'd to something still diviner
  Than mere language can impart :

Ever prompting—ever seeing
  Some improvement yet to plan;
To uplift our fellow being,
  And, like man, to feel for man!

What is noble ?—is the sabre
  Nobler than the humble spade ?—
There 's a dignity in labour,
  Truer than e'er Pomp arrayed !
He who seeks the Mind's improvement
  Aids the world in aiding Mind !
Every great commanding movement
  Serves not one, but all mankind.

O'er the Forge's heat and ashes,—
  O'er the Engine's iron head,—
Where the rapid shuttle flashes,
  And the spindle whirls its thread :
There is labour, lowly tending
  Each requirement of the hour,—
There is genius, still extending
  Science, and its world of power !

'Mid the dust, and speed, and clamour,
  Of the loom-shed and the mill;
'Midst the clink of wheel and hammer,
  Great results are growing still !
Though too oft, by Fashion's creatures,
  Work and workers may be blamed,
Commerce need not hide its features,—
  Industry is not ashamed !

What is noble ?—that which places
   Truth in its enfranchised will,
Leaving steps,—like angel-traces,
   That mankind may follow still !
E'en though Scorn's malignant glances
   Prove him *poorest* of his clan,
He's the *Noble*—who advances
   Freedom, and the Cause of Man !

WORK AND WIN.

A TTEND, oh, Man,
   Uplift the banner of thy kind,
   Advance the ministry of mind :
   The mountain height is free to climb,—
   Toil on,—MAN's heritage is TIME !
      Toil on !

   Work on and win :—
Life without work is unenjoyed ;
The happiest are the best employed !—
Work moves and moulds the mightiest birth,
And grasps the destinies of earth !
      Work on !

Work sows the seed;
Even the *rock* may yield its flower,—
No lot so hard, but human power,
Exerted to one end and aim,
May conquer fate, and capture fame !
        Press on !

Press onward still;
In nature's centre lives the fire
That slow, though sure, doth yet aspire;
Through fathoms deep of mould and clay,
It splits the rocks that bar its way !
        Press on !

If nature then
Lay tame beneath her weight of earth,
When would her hidden fire know birth?
Thus Man, through *granite* Fate, must find
The path,—the upward path,—of Mind !
        Work on !

Pause not in fear;
Preach no desponding, servile view,—
Whate'er thou will'st thy WILL may do !
Strengthen each manly nerve to bend
Truth's bow, and bid its shaft ascend !
        Toil on !

Be firm of heart;
By fusion of unnumber'd years
A *continent* its vastness rears !
A drop, 'tis said, through flint will wear;
Toil on, and Nature's conquest share !
Toil on !

Within thyself
Bright morn, and noon, and night succeed,—
Power, feeling, passion, thought and deed;
Harmonious beauty prompts thy breast,—
Things angels love, and God hath blest !
Work on !

Work on and win !
Shall light from Nature's depths arise,
And thou, whose mind can grasp the skies,
Sit down with Fate, and idly rail ?
No—onward ! Let the Truth prevail !
Work on !

ISABELLE DE CROYE.

ON, soldiers of St. Louis!—On, gallant youths
    of France !
Ride for the Boar of Ardennes—upon him with the
    lance !
Upon him—spur and spare not, until his blood be
    spilt ;—
And he—the curs'd of Heaven—lie as deep in gore
    as guilt !

Think of our noble Prelate—that white anointed
    brow,
All cloven by the brutal axe—and spur for Vengeance
    now !
Think of the murderer, De La Marck, and of his
    ruffian horde—
And on them, like a thunderbolt, with arrow, spear,
    and sword !

And fast and far—from hall and tower—prince, peer,
    and knight sweep by,
The banners of the fleur-de-lis rush, like a storm, on
    high !
And many an upward gaze is cast—as rank by rank
    march on,
Where crowd the fair and beauteous o'er the gateway
    of Peronne.

There, lovely as the face of morn, when light hath
    kissed its cheek,
And golden clouds around its brow in grace and
    beauty break ;
The love of every minstrel lute—the theme of every
    lay—
Fair Isabelle de Croye appeared, and bore all hearts
    away !

Yet she—for whom e'en royalty had sought, and sued
    in vain,—
She, whom the Prince of Orleans had perill'd life to
    gain ;
The shrine of every soldier's hope, the star of every
    glance,
Prefers a knight of Scotland to all the peers of France.

While swiftly 'neath the battlements, in chivalrous
    array,
Advance the spears of Crawford, of Crevecœur, and
    Dunois ;
The thoughtful cheek of Isabelle waxed pale as if
    with woe,
Till Quentin, and the Scottish guard, sprang forth in
    gallant show !

Then flushed her brow with crimson—then throbb'd
    her snowy breast—
And love, in every glance and grace, came beauteously
    confest ;

Oh, scarcely could her trembling breath the simplest
    word command,
When Quentin's favour'd lance convey'd a letter to
    her hand!

" Farewell, love, ne'er to see me more—or see me
    crown'd with fame!
To win thy hand I first must win a Hero's lofty
    name ;
And I have vowed by Scotia's saint!—by Honour's
    sacred shrine!
That yon bright orb shall see me dead—or Conquest
    see me thine!

" Farewell! thine hand is still the prize for which I
    venture all!
And if—oh, if—dear Isabelle, despite of hope, I fall!
Forget not 'mid the courtly throng, when others bend
    the knee,
The heart that 'mid the battle died—and died still
    loving thee!"

SPIRITUAL VISION.

A WANDERING of the soul, as though it
    dreamed;
A world of thought—a spirit kingdom found—
The immortal portion from its clay redeem'd,
    Reaching eternity at one bright bound!

A dream? a vision?—no, this gorgeous Night,
    These marvels beaming from a realm unknown,
Shine not without, *within* is all their light—
    A mystery mirror'd in the soul alone!

Within, we have Eternity within!—
    Yet, ever seeking, know not what we seek;
Possessing more than Prophets sought to win—
    Yet, feeling darkness, shrink—and dare not speak!

With hands stretched ever o'er that gloomy sphere,
    Dividing earth from heaven, where all seem fled;
We call—but from the void no voice, once dear,
    Brings us immortal accents from the dead!

The symbol of our hope dissolves away
    'Midst tombs, unmindful of their sacred trust,
We question ashes,—commune with decay,—
    And read Mankind's brief elegy—in dust!

The footsteps of a future doom we hear,
　Against whose coming nought may e'er avail;
And vague presentment of some evil near,
　Falls on our heart and turns its current pale.

We tread upon the verge of mighty things;
　We grasp the veil, but with unseeing mind;
Death hides the light, the soul, unconscious, brings—
　And on the edge of fate we wander blind.

Take thou a poet's counsel to thy heart,
　Question thy spirit; make its wisdom thine;
Shut out the world—pride, pomp, and every part,—
　As these retire—advance the worlds divine !—

Then spiritual loveliness appears;—
　God's nature glows in every form we see;
The *Mind's* the PROPHECY of *other* Spheres!
　And in Itself its own Futurity !—

Turn to thy soul, eternity is there;
　The key of the Invisible behold ;—
Spirit thou art, of Spirit-worlds the heir;
　All other secrets can thy Cross unfold !

THE MOTHER.

I.

A SOFTENING thought of other years,
  A feeling link'd to hours,
When Life was all too bright for tears,—
  And Hope sang, wreath'd with flowers!
A memory of affections fled—
  Of voices—heard no more!—
Stirred in my spirit when I read
  That name of fondness o'er!

II.

Oh *Mother!*—in that early word
  What loves and joys combine;
What hopes—too oft, alas!—deferr'd;
  What vigils—griefs—are thine!—
Yet, never, till the hour we roam—
  By worldly thralls opprest,
Learn we to prize that truest home—
  A watchful mother's breast!

III.

The thousand prayers at midnight pour'd
　　Beside our couch of woes;
The wasting weariness endured
　　To soften *our* repose !—
Whilst never murmur mark'd thy tongue—
　　Nor toils relaxed thy care :—
How, Mother, is thy heart so strong
　　To pity and forbear ?

IV.

What filial fondness e'er repaid
　　Or could repay the past ?—
Alas ! for gratitude decayed !
　　Regrets—that rarely last !—
'Tis only when the dust is thrown
　　Thy lifeless bosom o'er;
We muse upon thy kindness shown—
　　And wish we 'd loved thee more !

V.

'Tis only when thy lips are cold—
　　We mourn with late regret,
'Mid myriad memories of old—
　　The days for ever set !
And not an act—nor look—nor thought—
　　Against thy meek control,
But with a sad remembrance fraught
　　Wakes anguish in the soul !

On every land—in every clime—
    True to her sacred cause,
Fill'd by that effluence sublime
    From which her strength she draws,
Still is the Mother's heart the same—
    The Mother's lot as tried:—
Then, oh! may Nations guard that name
    With filial power and pride!

THE BRITISH BOW.

I.

HURRAH! the Bow, the British bow,
    The gallant, fine old English bow!
    Never flashed sword upon the foe,
    Like arrow from the good yew bow!
What knight a nobler weapon wields?
Thou victor of a thousand fields,—
Are lances, carbines, thy compeers?
No: vouch it, Cressy and Poictiers!
With hearts of oak and bows of yew,
And shafts that like the lightening flew,
Old England wore her proudest crown,
Nor bolt nor brand might strike it down!
                    Hurrah!

II.

Hurrah! the bow, the British bow,
The merry, true old English Bow!
Where fed the stag or sprung the roe,
There bent the ready stout yew bow!
What hoof of speed dared scorn its might?
What plume outsoar its glorious flight?
Oh! joyous was the greenwood then,
And matchless all her own bold men;
Her rovers rude by mount and flood,
Her king of outlaws, Robin Hood!
Right daring, reckless, wild, and free,
Great champion of the brave yew-tree,
　　　　　　　　　　　　Hurrah!

III.

Hurrah! the bow, the British bow,
The stately, firm old English bow!
What souls with freedom's spirit glow,
That love not thee, heroic bow?
When haughty Gaul deem'd all-secure
The victor's wreath at Agincourt,
Thy shafts, triumphant from the string,
Bore fate and vengeance on their wing;
And well the serried ranks might reel,
When, like a hurricane of steel,
They saw ten thousand barbs assail
Their horse and horsemen, helm and mail!
　　　　　　　　　　　　Hurrah!

IV.

Hurrah ! the bow, the British bow,
The graceful, light old English bow !
What island of the world may show
Aught like our own unconquer'd bow ?
The guardian of our native wild,
When Liberty was yet a child ;
Ere yet were launch'd our ships of war,
Our thunderbolts of Trafalgar ;
When Nelson was no magic word—
Drake, Hawke, St. Vincent's fame unheard !
Then, oh !—whilst freedom's bounties flow,
Thrice honour'd be the bow ! the bow !
    Old England's bow ! Hurrah !

TO THE NIGHT WIND.

I.

ART thou a lover, wandering the green lanes,
  And murmuring to thyself some legend old—
Strange tale of Night, from dungeon-tower and
   chains,
  Led by some spirit from the vaulted mould ?
Art thou a lover, through the moon's fond hours,
Fancying thy bride's cheek in the blushing flowers?

Or mourn'st thou now some faithful heart and dear,
    That in the churchyard gray thou stay'st so long;
Leaving upon the tall rank grass a tear,
    Sighing thy wild and melancholy song?
Art thou a mourner, thou mysterious Wind,
O'er beauty lost---affections left behind?

III

Or com'st thou from the distant vessel's side,
    With blessings laden, to the widow's cot?
Her Sailor-Boy! her buried husband's pride!
    Still his lone mother's home forgets he not?
Say; art thou herald of the thousand tongues
That pour on thee their joys, griefs, hopes, and
    wrongs?

Yes; sighs are on thee—musical as love;
    Hopes which are half immortal in their flight;
Joys which, like angels, waft the soul above;
    Wrongs that call heaven to vindicate the right!
The cherished secrets of each heart and mind
Lie bare to thee, thou unrecording wind?

v.

All things of earth are radiant with romance;
　A spiritual language breathes around!
Even thou, lone Wind! that touchest few perchance,
　Art still the very poetry of sound!
From thy soft rising to thy wildest hour,
Thou sing'st of life, eternity, and power!

THE OTHER DAY.

IT seems, love, but the other day
　Since thou and I were young together;
　And yet we 've trod a toilsome way,
　　And wrestled oft with stormy weather;
I see thee in thy spring of years,
　Ere cheek or curl had known decay;
And there 's a music in mine ears,
　As sweet as heard the other day!

Affection like a rainbow bends
　Above the past, to glad my gaze,
And something still of beauty lends
　To memory's dream of other days;
Within my heart there seems to beat
　That lighter, happier heart of youth,
When looks were kind, and lips were sweet,
　And love's world seemed a world of truth.

Within this inner heart of mine
    A thousand golden fancies throng,
And whispers of a time divine
    Appeal with half-forgotten tongue:
I know, I feel, 'tis but a dream,
    That thou art old and I am grey,
And that, however brief it seem,
    We are not as the other day.

Not as the other day—when flowers
    Shook fragrance on our joyous track;
When Love could never count the hours,
    And Hope ne'er dreamt of looking back:
When, if the world had been our own,
    We thought how changed should be its state,—
Then every cot should be a throne,
    The poor as happy as the great!—

When we'd that scheme which Love imparts,
    That chain all interests to bind —
The fellowship of human hearts,
    The federation of mankind!
And though with us time travels on,
    Still relics of our youth remain,
As some flowers, when their spring is gone,
    Yet late in autumn bloom again.

Alas ! 'mid worldly things and men,
    Love's hard to caution or convince;
And hopes, which were but fables then,
    Have left with us their moral since;

The Other Day.

The twilight of the memory cheers
    The soul with many a star sublime,
And still the mists of other years
    Hang dew-drops on the leaves of Time.

For what was then obscure and far
    Hath grown more radiant to our eyes,
Although the promised, hoped-for star
    Of social love hath yet to rise.
Still foot by foot the world is crost—
    Still onward, though it slow appear:
Who knows how slight a balance lost
    Might cast the bright sun from its sphere !

All time is lost in littleness !
    All time, alas ! if rightly shown,
Is but a shadow, more or less,
    Upon life's lowly dial thrown.
The greatest pleasures, greatest grief,
    Can never bear the test of years:
The pleasures vanish leaf by leaf,
    The sorrow wastes away in tears.

Then, though it seem a trifling space
    Since youth, and mirth, and hope were ours,
Yet those who love us most may trace
    The hand of age amid our flowers.
Thus day by day life's ages grow;
    The sands which hourly fall and climb
Mark centuries in their ceaseless flow,
    And cast the destinies of Time !

HUMAN' PROGRESS.

WE are told to look through Nature
    Upward unto Nature's God;
We are told there is a Scripture
    Written on the meanest sod;
That the simplest flower created
    Is a key to hidden things;
But, immortal over Nature,
    Mind, the lord of Nature, springs!

Through *Humanity* look upward,—
    Alter ye the olden plan,—
Look through Man to the Creator,
    Maker, Father, God of Man !—
Shall imperishable spirit
    Yield to perishable clay ?
No, sublime o'er Alpine mountains,
    Soars the Mind its heavenward way !—

Deeper than the vast Atlantic
    Rolls the tide of human thought;
Farther speeds that *mental* ocean
    Than the world of waves e'er sought!
Mind, sublime in its own essence,
    Its sublimity can lend
To the rocks, and mounts, and torrents,
    And, at will, their features bend !

Human Progress.

Some within the humblest *floweret*
  "Thoughts too deep for tears" can see;
Oh, the humblest *man* existing
  Is a sadder theme to me!
Thus I take the mightier labour,
  Of the great Almighty hand;
And through man to the Creator,
  Upward look, and weeping stand.

Thus I take the mightier labour,
  Crowning glory of *His* will;
And believe that in the meanest—
  Lives a spark of Godhead still:
Something that, by Truth expanded,
  Might be fostered into worth;
Something struggling through the darkness,
  Owning an immortal birth!

From the genesis of being
  Unto this imperfect day,
Hath Humanity held onward
  Praying God to aid its way!—
And Man's Progress had been swifter
  Had he never turned aside
To the worship of a symbol,
  Not the spirit signified!

And Man's progress had been higher
  Had he owned his brother man,
Left his narrow, selfish circle,
  For a world-embracing plan!

There are some for ever craving,
　Ever discontent with place,
In the eternal would find briefness,
　In the infinite want space.

If through man unto his Maker
　We the source of truth would find,
It must be thro' man enlightened—
　Educated, raised, refined:
That which the Divine hath fashioned.
　Ignorance hath oft effaced;
Never may we see God's image
　In man darken'd—man debased !—

Something yield to Recreation,
　Something to Improvement give;
There 's a Spiritual kingdom
　Where the Spirit hopes to live !
There 's a mental world of grandeur,
　Which the mind aspires to know;
Founts of everlasting beauty
　That, for those who seek them, flow !

Shores where Genius breathes immortal;
　Where the very winds convey
Glorious thoughts of Education,
　Holding universal sway !
Glorious hopes of Human Freedom,
　Freedom of the noblest kind;
That which springs from Cultivation,
　Cheers, and elevates the mind !

Let us hope for Better Prospects,—
  Strong to struggle for the right,
We appeal to Truth, and ever
  Truth's omnipotent in might;
Hasten then the People's progress,
  Ere their last faint hope be gone;
Teach the Nations, that their interest
  And the People's good, ARE ONE !

SOMETHING CHEAP.

THERE'S not a cheaper thing on earth,
  Nor yet one half so dear;
    'Tis worth more than distinguish'd birth,
    Or thousands gained a-year;
It lends the day a new delight;
  'Tis virtue's firmest shield;
And adds more beauty to the night
  Than all the stars may yield.

It maketh poverty content,
  To sorrow whispers peace;
It is a gift from Heaven sent
  For mortals to increase:
It meets you with a smile at morn;
  It lulls you to repose;
A flower for peer and peasant born,
  An everlasting rose.

A charm to banish grief away,
  To snatch the frown from care;
Turn tears to smiles, make dulness gay—
  Spread gladness everywhere:
And yet 'tis cheap as summer dew,
  That gems the lily's breast;
A talisman for love, as true
  As ever man possess'd.

As smiles the rainbow through the cloud
  When threatening storm begins—
As music 'mid the tempest loud,
  That still its sweet way wins—
As springs an arch across the tide,
  Where waves conflicting foam,
So comes this seraph to our side,
  This angel of our home.

What may this wondrous spirit be,
  With power unheard before—
This charm, this bright divinity?
  Good temper—nothing more!
Good temper!—'tis the choicest gift
  That woman homeward brings,
And can the poorest peasant lift
  To bliss unknown to kings.

LIKING AND DISLIKING.

YE, who know the reason, tell me
    How it is that instinct still
Prompts the heart to like—or like not—
    At its own capricious will?
Tell me by what hidden magic
    Our impressions first are led
Into liking—or disliking—
    Oft before a word is said?

Why should *smiles* sometimes repel us,—
    Bright eyes turn our feelings cold?
What *is* that which comes to tell us
    All that glitters is not gold?
Oh! no feature, plain or striking,
    But a power we cannot shun,
Prompts our liking—or disliking—
    Ere acquaintance hath begun!

Is it instinct,—or some spirit
    Which protects us, and controls
Every impulse we inherit
    By some sympathy of souls?
Is it instinct,—is it nature,—
    Or some freak or fault of chance,
Which our liking—or disliking—
    Limits to a single glance?

Like presentiment of danger,
 Though the sky no shadow flings,
Or that inner sense, still stranger,
 Of unseen, unutter'd things !
Is it—oh ! can no one tell me,—
 No one show sufficient cause,
Why our likings—and dislikings—
 Have their own instinctive laws ?

THE VOICE OF NIGHT.

I.

HOW beautiful the heavens look to-night !—
 So calm, transparent; and the starry crowd,—
Those exquisite embodiments of light,—
Could ye not almost fancy they were proud
Of their own loveliness ?—that they had bliss
In beaming forth on such a night as this ?

II.

For ever and for ever there is set
In the enduring sky, a seal and sign,
A voiceless evidence of God !—which yet
Unchanged shall live, when this frail form of mine
Hath mouldered from the bosom of the earth,
Leaving no record of its mortal birth.

III.

The *elements* of which we are composed
May perish; *they* are finite: but the soul
Bursts from the frame in which it lived enclosed,
Beyond the grasping reach of Time's control!—
That spirit which within us swells and speaks,
Shall *find* the immortality it *seeks /*

IV.

Oh, thou !—Creator !—God !—and can it be
That man is heir to thine own glorious heaven ?—
'Tis so !—the *light*, which is *sublimity*,—
The *essence*, which is *thought*, by Thee were given !—
The fear and heaviness of doubt are o'er—
I muse, and feel—and tremble—and adore !

REBECCA.

———

UPON the parapet she leapt;
    And stood in her heroic woe
Like one that Heaven's own hand still kept
    From dashing down the void below!
She stood—she look'd—like one inspired;
    Decision mark'd her very breath;
That heart which Honour's voice had fired
    Could seek the verge – and smile at death !

Stand back—she cried—thou craven knight—
  Thou man debased—thou priest forsworn—
Stand back ! or thus before thy sight
  I leap—and laugh thy power to scorn !
Think'st thou a woman's soul can be
So helpless in its purity ?
That earth has lent to *Guilt* alone
A strength to Innocence unknown ?
Turn, baffled traitor, turn and find
No weakness sways the immortal mind !
My strength is yet in Abraham's God !
  My faith is still enthroned above;
Better to die where truth hath trod,
  Than live polluted by thy love !

THE SLUMBERERS.

I.

GAZE thou upon this mental dome—
  This mortal palace of the mind—
  This spirit-dwelling—this soul's home—
    To dreamy slumber now resigned:
The fringed and ivory doors are closed
  Upon the azure world below;
The ruby hall, where Love reposed,
  Hath lost its soft, its minstrel flow.
To the land of dreams hath fled
Music sweet as incense shed !

II.

Tranquil rest the small white feet;
   How unmoved the graceful hand !
Yet, in measured circle's fleet
   Dance they in the visioned land !
Calmly, as the frozen snow,
   O'er her arm of beauty rare,
Droops that pale enchanted brow
   'Neath its long and shadowy hair;
Not a smile the lip surrounds,
Yet she laughs where mirth abounds !

III.

Round the damask curtains fall,
   Soft the silken pillow bends,
Nothing save the watcher's call
   To the ear Time's echo lends;
Yet, beneath the living green
   Of the ancient woods and hills,
Where the timid fawns are seen
   Trooping by the forest rills;
Thousand flowers around her beaming,
Walks she in the land of dreaming !

IV.

Strange that the *closed* eye should see !—
   That the *stirless* feet should dance
To a magic minstrelsy,
   Heard but in the sleeper's trance.

Strange the *voiceless* lip should sing !
    That the curtain fold on high,
With the branching leaves of spring,
    Should delude the Dreamer's eye!
Mirthful—yet without a smile !
Mute—yet singing all the while.

*   *   *   *   *

V.

To a darker couch we tread,
    Where a maiden lowly lies;
Solemn light the tapers shed,
    O'er the cold and shrouded eyes !
On her white, unheaving breast,
    As the sculptor's marble fair,
One pale, wasted hand doth rest,
    Half upcurved as still in prayer :
To the land of souls have flown
Feelings sweet as angels' own.

VI.

Mark how wan the sombre brow !
    Sadly dark the fallen cheeks;
Yet, she soars a seraph now,
    Where the morn of Heaven breaks.

Silent in her virgin shroud,
   Silent on her funeral bed;
Like a lily crushed and bowed,
   Ere its brief spring-hour had fled:
Silent—yet she sings—she hears
The host of God's seraphic spheres !

VII.

Strange the lifeless eye should know
   Glories hid from living gaze;
Strange that form of saddest wo
   Lifts to God rejoicing praise.
Strange that hand so meekly laid
   On the sunk and wearied breast,
Clasped by Christ—in Faith arrayed—
   Is guided to immortal rest.
Lost—yet with Jehovah found !
Dead—yet with the deathless crowned !

THE FISHERMAN'S CHILDREN.

I.

SLOWLY the melancholy day,
   In cloud and storm passed o'er;
Fearful and wild the tall ships lay,
   Off the rude Northumbrian shore;
'Mid the thunder's crash—and the lightning's ray,
   And the dashing ocean's roar!

II.

And many a father's heart beat high,
   With an aching fear of wo:
As he gazed upon the ghastly sky,
   And heard the tempest blow!
Or watched with sad and anxious eye,
   The warring waves below!

III.

Oh! many a mournful mother wept;
   And closer, fonder prest
The babe that soft and sweetly slept
   Upon her troubled breast;
While every hour that lingering crept,
   Her agonies confest!

IV.

And *one* upon her couch was laid,
   In deep and helpless pain;
Two children sought her side, and played,
   And strove to cheer—in vain:
Till breathlessly, and half afraid,
   They listened to the rain!

V.

"'Tis a rough sea your father braves!"
   The afflicted mother said;
" Pray that the Holy arm that saves,
   May guard his precious head!
May shield him from the wrecking waves,
   To aid ye, when I'm dead!"

VI.

Then low the children bended there,
   With clasped hands, to implore
That God would save them from despair,
   And their loved sire restore:
And the heavens *heard* that quiet prayer,
   'Mid all the tempest's roar!

VII.

'Twas eve!—and cloudlessly at last,
   The sky in beauty gleamed!
O'er snowy sail and lofty mast
   The painted pennon streamed;
The danger and the gloom had passed,
   Like horrors—*only dreamed!*

VIII.

Swift to the desolated beach
  The Fisher's children hied ;
But far as human sight could reach,
  No boat swept o'er the tide !
Still on they watched—and with sweet speech,
  To banish grief they tried !

IX.

Long, long they sat—when, lo! a light
  And distant speck was seen,—
Small as the smallest star of night,
  When night is most serene !—
But to the Fisher's boy that sight
  A sight of bliss had been !

X.

" It comes !" he cried, " our father's boat !
  See !—sister—by yon stone !
Not there—not there—still more remote—
  I know the sail's our own !
Look !—look again !—they nearer float !
  Thanks !—thanks to God alone !"

XI.

Four happy, grateful hearts were those,
  That met at even-fall ;
The mother half forgot her woes,
  And kissed and blessed them all !
" Praised ! praised," she said, " be He who shows
  Sweet mercy when we call !"

TENT OF ABRAHAM.

THE shadows of an eastern day
 Lengthened along the sandy way,—
When, toiling faint and lone,
An aged wanderer cross'd the plain,—
As if his every step were pain,
 His every breath a groan !
Till Abraham's tent appear'd in view,
And slowly towards its rest he drew.

And Abraham met his way-worn look
With pity,—for the old man shook
 With years, at every tread ;
For he the wrinkled impress bore
Of full one hundred years, or more,
 Upon his silvery head ;
Then Abraham washed his aching feet,—
Assauged their pain,—and brought him meat.

Ye should have known the burning glare
Of soil, and sun, and sultry air,
    To tell how sweet the draught
That bless'd those lips, so parch'd and old;
Oh ! water,—not a world of gold
    Could buy the joy he quaff'd !
Ye should have toiled the burning waste
To know how sweetly food can taste !

But Abraham saw, with deep amaze,
The old man's strange and godless ways;
    For ere he bent to eat,
Nor praise, nor thanks, he utter'd there,
Nor raised his grateful eyes in prayer
    To God who sent him meat;
Sudden he sat in eager mood,
And call'd no blessing on the food !—

"Owneth thou not the God of Heaven,
That unto thee these things hath given ?"
    Said Abraham, in his ire;
He answer'd,—" Five score years I've trod,
Yet worshipp'd but one only God,—
    The eternal God of Fire !"
And Abraham wroth, his anger spent,
And thrust him, storming, from his tent !

Then there was sudden awe on Night,—
The pale west quivered with wild light,
　　The stars apart were thrown;
And all the air around the sky
Seem'd like a glory hung on high,—
　　A gleam of worlds unknown;
And from that glory, high install'd,
A voice,—God's voice,—to Abraham call'd !

" Why went the Stranger from thy board !"
And Abraham answer'd,—" Know, O Lord,
　　That he denied Thy name;
Neither would worship Thee, nor bless:
So forth, unto the wilderness,
　　I drove him, in his shame !"
And God said,—" If *I* still allow
Peace to his errors,—could'st not thou ?

" If I, these hundred years have borne
This wanderer's sin, neglect, and scorn,
　　Yet ne'er did vengeance seek,
How is 't that thou, *for one poor night,*
Could'st bear him not within thy sight ?—
　　Look up to me,—and speak !"
Then towards the Voice, with trembling steps, he
　　trod,
And Abraham stood rebuked before his God.

THERE ARE TWO WAYS TO LIVE
ON EARTH.

THERE are two ways to live on earth,—
　　Two ways to judge,—to act,—to view;
For all things here have double birth,—
　　A right and wrong,—a false and true !

Give me the home where kindness seeks
　　To make that sweet which seemeth small;
Where every lip in fondness speaks,
　` And every mind hath care for all.

Whose inmates live in glad exchange
　　Of pleasures, free from vain expense;
Whose thoughts beyond their means ne'er range,
　　Nor wise denials give offence !

Who in a neighbour's fortune find
　　No wish,—no impulse,—to complain;
Who feel not,—never felt,—the mind
　　To envy yet another's gain !

Who dream not of the mocking tide
　　Ambition's foil'd endeavour meets,—
The bitter pangs of wounded pride,
　　Nor fallen Power, that shuns the streets.

Though Fate deny its glitt'ring store,
   Love's wealth is still the wealth to choose;
For all that Gold can purchase more
   Are gauds, it is no loss to lose!

Some beings, wheresoe'er they go,
   Find nought to please, or to exalt,—
Their constant study but to show
   Perpetual modes of finding fault.

While others, in the ceaseless round
   Of daily wants, and daily care,
Can yet cull flowers from common ground,
   And *twice* enjoy the joy they *share!*

Oh! happy they who happy *make,*—
   Who, *blessing,* still themselves are blest!—
Who something spare for others' sake,
   And strive, in all things, for the best!

THE SCHOONER.

I.

THE misty sun sank fast
　　O'er the long and gloomy main,
And the hollow moaning blast
　Swept like a burial strain.

II.

Yet swift the vessel flew,
　In the spirit of her pride;
And the surges dashed like dew
　From her bold, majestic side!

III.

The dim horizon shed
　A thin and sickly ray;
The dull, black vapours spread
　Like a pall along her way.

IV.

Yet lovely 'midst the storm—
　As a rainbow on the deep—
Did the Schooner's stately form
　O'er the bursting billows sweep!

V.

Blacker and blacker set
  The wild, portentous night;
The winds and waters met,
  Like demons in their might.

VI.

The tempest rode the main,
  With death-denouncing speed;
And the giànt mast was snapt in twain,
  As a child would break a reed!

VII.

Then paler fell the cheek—
  And dimmer grew the sight—
And lips that wished, yet dared not speak,
  Turned cold and ghastly white.

VIII.

On—on the vessel ran,—
  Trembling, and wild, and bare—
The skill and strength of man
  Were dust upon the air.

IX.

On—on the vessel burst—
  No helm—no cheering ray—
Like a dying thing accurst,
  She held her dreadful way!

X.

The breakers girt her round;
    One fierce wild shout of fear—
And the roaring waves were the only sound
    That reached the landsman's ear!

    *   *   *   *   *

XI.

'Twas a blue and moonlight night,
    With a mild and shoreward breeze;
When a lonely wreck hove first in sight,
    On the far Ægean seas.

XII.

No signal sound arose
    From the solitary deck;
She seem'd alone amidst her foes—
    That miserable wreck!

XIII.

From helm to prow no sound
    Of living thing was there;—
Some gallant crew a grave had found,
    Unblest by earthly prayer!

XIV.

Deep silence reigned above;
    But, ah!—the berth below
Displayed a scene of human love—
    A scene of human wo!

XV.

The beautiful—alas!—
  The bright—the better flower
Is ever thus the first to pass
  From Love's domestic bower!

XVI.

A youth, in sickness deep,
  Lay breathing weak and low,
As soon the everlasting sleep
  Would settle on his brow.

XVII.

And there—in all the pride
  Of early bloom and grace,
A fair-haired girl knelt by his side,
  With meekly beauteous face.

XVIII.

With blue, beseeching eyes,
  In stedfast hope upraised!—
She seemed a sister of the skies,—
  So holy was that gaze!

XIX.

And smote the hand of Death
  Thus mildly in its might?
Lived there on that sweet lip no breath—
  In those blue eyes no light?

XX.

Oh! lovely and not dark,
  Death, is thy mild decay,
When the immortal spark
  Yet radiates our clay!

XXI.

A gleam of daylight set,
  May gild the cloud of eve;
And the soul's light linger yet
  O'er the form it sighed to leave!

XXII.

Serene she knelt in *death*,
  Beside the sufferer's bed;
The youth lay warm with life's free breath!—
  The weary watcher dead!

FAIRIES AND FLOWERS.

I.

FROM the bright chambers of the vestal rose
  No more the fairies to their revels bound;
The lily's ivory halls no more disclose
Their elfin tribe—nor fays, with goss'mer crowned,
Slow float on silver blossoms to the ground:
No more we hear their viewless minstrels play,
As when in emerald rings they danced around,—
The vision and the grace have left our day,
And England's fairy world passed, with *its youth*, away!

II.

The bright mythology of vanished days!—
We are too learn'd its credence to allow;
Science hath oped too wide our colder gaze :—
But are we better—wiser—happier—now
That we fair fancy's birth-right disavow?—
No more believe the midnight eyes behold
Shapes. born of air, to which the planets bow?
No longer seek the fairy palace old
Which elves chivalrous guard, with straw-like spears
    of gold.

III.

Hither, ye fays!—fantastic elves!—that leap
The slender hare-cup,—climb the cowslip bells—
And teaze the wild bee as she lies asleep!
Hither from shrines of bloom, and glow-worm
  cells,—
From leafy halls—and flowery citadels,—
Hither, bright fairies;—hither to my breast!
Lead me once more where childhood's memory
  dwells
In its believing beauty—heaven imprest!—
Bring innocence and faith,—be each again my guest!

IV.

Visions of immortality!—that show
The longing of the mind for something more
Than mortal being!—the deep wish to know
The things of other worlds,—the angel store
Of mystery learnt but on the spirit-shore,
Where mid-way fairies sport on fancy's track!—
Glad elves! our season of romance restore,—
Come, our Aladdin-years we'll wander back,—
See fairy-hunters gay, and their bold insect-pack!

V.

We have breasts, now, in which affections dead
Have left their "withered rings" around the heart!
And bosoms whence the child of hope hath fled,
Although no fairy in its loss had part!

The cup o'erturned, though by no elfin art !
The rifled chalice, and the broken bowl,
Where memory by the fount whence sorrows start,
Keeps green the old mythology of soul,—
Those fairy realms of youth o'er which Time's death-
    wheels roll !—

VI.

Have *we* not tasted of the fairy dew?—
Do *we* behold things as they *really* are ?
Or, like Titania, gaze with spell bound view,
And lavish love on what were best afar ?—
Proves *that* not oft a stone, we deemed a star !—
Alas, each bosom hath its Oberon too ;—
Susceptibility—which seeks to war
With what it loves, and most desires to woo ;
Yet urged—unknowing why—to wound, and still
    pursue !

VII.

Oh, Queen of Fancy, what an empire's thine !—
What classic loveliness pervades thy shore !—
Creations which the bard hath made divine—
Idols and gods—all creeds alike adore—
The mental deities of ages hoar ;
Harmonious moulds where deathless pæans sound
Sole consecrate to genius evermore !—
Where every step finds intellectual ground,
Thronged by the kings of mind, that time, and fame
    have crowned.

VIII.

Have not the flowers a language? Speak, young *rose*,
Speak, bashful sister of the footless dell!
Thy blooming loves,—thy sweet regards disclose;
Oh, speak!—for many a legend keep'st thou well;
Old tales of wars—crusading knights who fell,
And bade thee minister their latest sighs!—
Speak, grayhaired *daisy!*—ancient *primrose*, tell!
Ye, vernal harps! ye, sylvan harmonies!—
Speak, poets of the fields!—rapt gazers on the skies!

THEY ARE NO MORE.

THEY are no more!   O, dull and drear,
 Sound those bereaving, mournful words;
Affliction finds no wilder tear—
 Memory no darker doom records;
Not in our homes, not by our side,
 Move the bright beings we deplore;
The hearts which love had sanctified,
     They are no more!

Oh, breathes there one that hath not known
 The parting word—the dying look—
While in the soul grief walked alone,
 And every pulse with anguish shook:

Some cherished one that blessed him there—
  And passed—as sunlight from the shore?
Woe! woe! the young—the loved—the fair—
        They are no more!

The music of their lips hath fled,
  Their grace and beauty passed away;
Yet lives the presence of the dead
  Within our souls, as light in day!
A fresher light shall burst the tomb,
  And all the blesséd lost restore;
Unknown those words of wail and gloom—
        They are no more!

THE VILLAGE QUEEN.

THE nuts hang ripe upon the chestnut boughs;
  And the rich stars send forth their clear blue light,
O'er glistening leaves, and flowers that, fond as love,
Perfume the very dew that bows their heads,
And lays their sweet and quiet beauty low!
And dream-like voices float upon the ear,
With mingling harmony of birds and trees,
And gushing waters! Beautiful is night—
And beautiful the *thoughts* she calls to birth!—

The *hopes* which make themselves immortal wing;
The *memories* that slow and sadly steal,
Like moonlight music, o'er the watching heart;
Yet, with a tone thus light, stirring the mind
To themes beyond a trumpet's breath to rouse !

My spirit wakes 'mid sad remembrances
Of one who shone the beauty of our vale—
The idol of our homes—our Village Queen !
Methinks I see her now !—the graceful girl !
The shadowy richness of her auburn hair
Half parted o'er a brow white as the bloom
Of the wild myrtle flower: and eyes whose hue
Was like the violet's, with more of light;
A silent poetry dwelt in their depths—
A melody inaudible !—Her neck—
Oh, elegant and fair as the young dove's !—
Gave to the mild expression of her form
The grace that artists study.   Thus she looked,
Ere early blight had wasted her fine bloom,
And dimmed the gladness of her starry eyes !
Her home was small but very beautiful:
A pastoral cot—midst mountain, rock, and vale,
And pleasant water—all that constitutes
A picture of romance—a summer home !
There, like a rose, she grew from infancy,
The blessing of a widowed mother's heart—
Light of her eyes—the dial of her mind,
Round which her thoughts revolved !

An orphan youth,

The offspring of a distant relative,
Dwelt with the aged matron and her child,
And rose to manhood 'neath their generous roof:
Alas, for the return !—'Tis strange that one
So mild and gentle in her loveliness,
Whose life was simple as the wilding broom,
And happiest in the shade, should nurse so fond,
So deep a passion for a youth whose moods
Were ever wayward, gloomy, wild, and bold,
Jealous and proud—the passionate reverse
Of her sweet, guileless self !   And *yet* she loved,
With that intense affection, that deep faith,
Which knows no change, and sets but o'er the tomb !
'Twere vain to trace how, step by step, he fell—
How, deed by deed, he darkened into *guilt*,
And perished in his crimes !

Sweet Eleanor !—

Pale, blighted girl !—she withered fast, like those
Who have no *earthly* hope; yet still she smiled,
And said she should be happy soon—and breathed,
Like a young dying swan, her music tones
Of parting tenderness, into that fount
Which might not hold them long—a mother's heart !

Oh ! youth is like the *emerald*, which throws
Its own *green* light o'er all !—even to the last,
She spoke of brighter hours, of happier days,

Of nights that bring no sorrow—no regret;
That she would love *none* but her mother now,
And *she* henceforth should be the world to her.

Do you behold where the lone rising moon
Tinges with holy light the village spire,
And braids with silver the far cypress boughs,
Bending, like Mercy, o'er the sorrowing brow,
And lonely heart, the weary and the worn?—
There, in her early tomb, reclines the pride
And beauty of our vale—The Village Queen!

BOYHOOD.

I.

THE dreams of early youth,
　　How beautiful they are—how full of joy—
When fancy looks like truth,
　　And life shews not a taint of sin's alloy.

II.

　　When every heart appears
The temple of high thought and noble deed—
　　When our most bitter tears
Fall o'er some melancholy page we read.

III.

The summer morn's fresh hours—
Her thousand woodland songs—her glorious hues:
Oh ! life's so full of flowers,
The difficulty *then*, is where to choose !

IV.

The wonderful blue sky—
Its cloudy palaces—its gorgeous fanes—
The rainbow tints which lie
Like distant golden seas near purple plains,—

V.

These never shine again,
As once they shone upon our raptured gaze :
The clouds which may remain
Paint *other visions* than in those sweet days !

VI.

In hours thus pure—sublime—
Dreams we would make realities : life seems
So changed in after-time,
That we would wish realities were dreams !

A LOVE-DREAM.

BY the village hawthorn seated
　　Waits a village maiden fair;
In her ear are sounds repeated
　　She hath heard elsewhere.
Why hath happiness such fleetness,
　　Wings that never rest?
When did memory's words of sweetness
　　Dwell in sweeter breast?

Lonely lies the field before her
　　In the twilight hour,
Yet the face of her adorer
　　Smiles from leaf and flower.
Inward is her loving vision,
　　Inward lists she to her heart;
In a world of thought Elysian,
　　Where time has no part.

Lost in dreams of tender feeling,
　　She forgets her cottage birth;
Lost in all love's fond revealing,
　　She is far from earth.
Truly but she dreameth greatly,
　　Nobly doth the maiden fare;
She is in a mansion stately
　　Wedded lady to the heir!

Wake her not—too soon love waketh—
  Soon is lost its world of dreams;
Like a golden bubble, breaketh
  All that most enduring seems!
Brighter heaven her soul is seeing
  In her trance than aught above;
Lost the whole of outward being
  In the inward life of love!

THE CHILD AND THE ANGELS.

THE Sabbath-sun was setting slow,
    Amidst the clouds of even;
"Our Father,"—breathed a voice below—
  "Father, who art in Heaven!"

Beyond the earth—beyond the cloud—
  Those infant words were given;
"Our Father,"—angels sang aloud—
  "Father, who art in Heaven!

"Thy kingdom come"—still from the ground,
  That child-like voice did pray;
"Thy kingdom come"—God's hosts resound—
  Far up the starry way!

" Thy will be done,"—with little tongue,
  That lisping love implores;
" Thy will be done,"—the angelic throng—
  Sing from seraphic shores !

" For ever,"—still those lips repeat,
  Their closing evening prayer;
" For ever,"—floats in music sweet—
  High 'midst the angels there !

THE LOST.

THE lost ! oh, what are they, the dead ?
    Alas, there *is* a grave
  To which the many Lost have fled,
    We might, yet would not save !
Lost time, which never more can be ;
  Lost joys, whose sun hath set;
Lost friends, whose tomb is Memory,
  Whose memory is Regret !

How like a churchyard is the heart,
  By buried relics crossed;
The *dead* are but a tithe, a part
  Of what the Heart hath lost !

The dead have an immortal dower,
　O'er which the soul may muse;
But, oh, the Lost! there's not an hour
　We live yet nothing lose!

Ah, me! the mystery of fate,
　The sorrow and the thrall,
How quick we learn to estimate
　What we can ne'er recall!
Lost hope, that, like an arkless dove,
　Hath fled this world of care;
Lost peace, lost happiness, lost love,
　Dispers'd, like things of air!

Yon sphere that shines from earth so far
　Finds yet some earthly trace;
How many a loved and lofty star
　Hath perished from its face!
Oh, stars of heaven! and can *ye* fall?
　Can ye by storms be tossed?
Alas for hope! alas for all
　We loved, and we have lost!

E'en Nature for her Woods deplores,
　Earth for her Cities gone,
Ocean for empires, and for shores
　O'er which her tides sweep on!
Nor heaven, nor earth, nor man, escapes,
　Nor element, nor clime;
All bow before that Hand which shapes
　The mysteries of time!

LOVE'S REMONSTRANCE.

I.

WHAT! for a word—an idle word?
    And more in jest than earnest spoken?
Were I to note each breath I heard
    My heart would soon be changed—or broken!
'Tis not when words are *sweetest* said,
    Love's living flower blooms there to meet us;
The flower of love may still be dead,
    Although its *fragrance* seem to greet us!
Then weigh not thou a word so slight,
    Nor keep thy gentle bosom grieving;
The tongue that finds things ever right,
    Believe me, love, 's a tongue deceiving.

II.

Oh, if my heart had sought thee less,
    Mine eyes loved less to wander round thee,
That word of wounded tenderness—
    That hasty word had never found thee.
The *dew* that seeks the Sun's fond gaze,
    His golden lips in gladness beaming;
Meets death within his *smiling* rays—
    His gilded fondness is but *seeming!*
Then weigh not thou a word so slight
    Nor keep thy gentle bosom grieving;
The tongue that finds things ever right,
    Believe me, love, 's a tongue deceiving.

THE HOME-BOUND BARK.

I.

'TIS the winter deep !
  And the sea-fowl sweep
    Afar o'er the gloomy tide;
And the wild waves dash,
'Neath the signal's flash,
  Where the foamy tempests ride.

II.

And dark and drear,
On the seaman's ear,
  Hang's the vulture's ravening cry;
Like the startling breath,
Of some fiend of death,
  In wait for the souls that die.

III.

The sails are rent—
The stout mast's bent—
  And the helm and bowsprit gone;
And fast and far,
'Midst the billowy war,
  The foundering bark drives on.

IV.

The shriek and prayer,
And the wan despair,
  Of hearts thus torn away,
Are seen and heard
By the ravening bird
  In chase of his drowning prey.

V.

Oh, many a sire,
By the low red fire,
  Will wake through this night of wo —
For those who sleep
'Neath the surges deep,
  Ten thousand fathom low !—

VI.

And many a maid,
In the lonely glade,
  For their absent love deplore ;
And watch and wail
For the home-bound sail
  No sun will see return !

VII.

Mourn not for the dead,
On their sandy bed,
  Nor their last long sleep deplore ;
But mourn for those,
In their home of woes,
  Who weep for evermore !

THE PEASANTRY OF ENGLAND.

I.

THE Peasantry of England,
    The merry hearts and free;
    The sword may boast a braver band—
    But give the scythe to me!
Give me the fame of industry,
    Worth all your classic tomes!
God guard the English Peasantry,
    And grant them happy homes!

II.

The sinews of old England!
    The bulwarks of the soil!
How much we owe each manly hand,
    Thus fearless of its toil!
Oh, he who loves the harvest free,
    Will sing where'er he roams,
God bless the English Peasantry,
    And give them happy homes!

III.

God speed the plough of England!
We'll hail it with three cheers;
And here's to those whose labour planned
The all which life endears!
May still the wealth of Industry
Be seen where'er man roams;
A cheer for England's Peasantry!
God send them happy homes!

THE BLIND BOY DYING.

MOTHER—Sister—are ye near me?
I awake with closèd eyes;
Eyes still dark—but let me hear ye—
Bless the blind boy, ere he dies!
Is the snow-drop come? dear mother,
Oh! I thought at its last birth
I should never hold another
Snow-drop in my hand on earth!

Something ever in its springing
Seemed my very heart to touch;
June, with all its roses bringing,
Never made me weep so much!

The Blind Boy Dying.

'Twas a sympathy, a feeling
   I could scarcely understand;
When I 've felt the tear-drop stealing
   O'er the snow-drop in my hand.

So, when I am dead, dear Mother,
   When your poor blind boy is gone;
Let the snow-drop, and no other,
   Rest his little shroud upon.
It shall go with me to heaven—
   It shall bloom at Jesu's feet—
And, when God my sight hath given,
   It my vision first shall meet.

Weep not, mother!—Though I'm weeping,
   There 's no sorrow in my tears.
Should I mourn to wake from sleeping
   In those sight-restoring spheres?
Yet I love—so love—that blindness,
   Sweet is here, as sight above!
Seraphs cannot show thy kindness,
   Angels cannot match thy love.

No: there is but one—one mother;
   Earth but one such heart can find;
And I know thou 'lt love no other
   As thou lov'st thine own—thy blind!

And I know each Sabbath morning
  Thou my grave wilt bend before,
With some flower its stone adorning,
  Though I ne'er can thank thee more.

Oft the sunlight will be stealing
  O'er my dark, cold, burial home,
Like a glance of God revealing
  Tidings of a world to come.
Oft the summer birds will warble,
  Warble sweetly as of yore;
Whilst these lips lie mute as marble—
  All their sighs and sufferings o'er!

Oh, sometimes, I shiver, mother—
  Shudder at the thought of death,
But I strive and strive to smother
  That which trembles on my breath:
God will keep me, God will aid me,
  He will calm this timorous mood;
For in all I have obeyed thee,
  Sought, dear mother, to be good.

Clasp me closer,—closer,—nearer;
  Lift my throbbing head more high;
Oh! I love you dearer, dearer,
  Every moment that I die!
When in heaven my God hath given
  Sight, where blindness now hath place,
It will be a second Heaven
  There to *see* my Mother's face.

SABBATH CHIMES.

THERE'S music in the morning air,
 A holy voice and sweet,
  Far calling to the House of Prayer
  The humblest peasant's feet.
From hill, and vale, and distant moor,
 Long as the chime is heard,
Each cottage sends its tenants poor
 For God's enriching Word.

Where'er the British power hath trod,
 The cross of faith ascends,
And, like a radiant arch of God,
 The light of Scripture bends !
Deep in the forest wilderness
  The *wood-built church* is known ;
A sheltering wing, in man's distress,
 Spread like the Saviour's own !

The warrior from his armed tent,
 The seaman from the tide,
Far as the Sabbath chimes are sent
 In Christian nations wide,—
Thousands and tens of thousands bring
 Their sorrows to His shrine,
And taste the never-failing spring
 Of Jesus' love divine !

If, at an *earthly* chime, the tread
   Of million, million feet
Approach whene'er the Gospel's read
   In God's own temple-seat,
How blest the sight, from Death's dark sleep,
   To see God's saints arise;
And countless hosts of angels keep
   The Sabbath of the skies !

THE ESCAPED CONVICT.

I.

HE trod his native land,
   The bright land of the free;
His forehead wore a seared brand—
   Impress of infamy !
His brow—where youth and beauty met—
Yes, there the seal of guilt was set.

II.

He gaz'd upon the vale,
   Where spring-tide flow'rets slept,
Rock'd by the whispers of the gale;
   He saw it—and he wept :
Like drops which page a storm they came,
Tears born in agony and shame.

III.

Morn sat upon the hills,
    But she look'd cold and dim,
Clouds, like a pall which death conceals,
    Hung frowning there on him :
All, e'en his lov'd, his mother land,
Scowl'd on his forehead and the brand.

IV.

My sire ! my sire ! he groan'd;
    My home! my lovely one !
What sire ? he hath his child disown'd—
    What home ? I—I have none:
I hear all curse—I see all shun :
Yet curse not thou—not thou—thy son !

V.

I saw *her* struck, whose cheek
    Did myriad sweets disclose;
Whose eyes, whose form—but wherefore speak—
    I saw !—my heart-blood rose :—
She loved me, she was sworn my bride—
I stabb'd the striker, and he died !—

VI.

For this—the record lies
    Fest'ring upon my brow;
For this—the rabble mock'd my cries;
    For this—shame haunts me now ;
For this—half rotted I must be,
Ere my dead brow from stain is free.

VII.

My own, my beauteous land,
　　Land of the brave—the high;
I ask'd but this of fate's stern hand—
　　To see thee—and to die !—
O ! yes, my country, let me be
In my last hour—in death—with thee.

VIII.

The moon look'd on the vale,
　　Wearing her starry wreath,
And soft display'd a form, that, pale
　　Lay there alone—with death:
The zephyrs drew a length'ned sigh,
And slow the convict's corse pass'd by.

IX.

"Twas said that lovely night
　　A spirit youth was seen
Gliding among the flow'rets bright,
　　The trees, and meadows green;
And chiefly by a cot, and there
It wept, and melted into air.

THE DEATH OF THE WARRIOR KING.

I.

THERE are noble heads bow'd down and pale,
  Deep sounds of woe arise,
And tears flow fast around the couch
  Where a wounded warrior lies;
The hue of death is gathering dark
  Upon his lofty brow,
And the arm of might and valour falls
  Weak as an infant's now.

II.

I saw him 'mid the battling hosts,
  Like a bright and leading star,
Where banner, helm, and falchion gleam'd.
  And flew the bolts of war:
When, in his plenitude of power,
  He trod the Holy Land,
I saw the routed Saracens
  Flee from his blood dark brand.

III.

I saw him in the banquet hour
    Forsake the festive throng,
To seek his favourite minstrel's haunt,
    And give his soul to song:
For dearly as he loved renown,
    He loved that spell-wrought strain
Which bade the brave of perished days
    Light conquest's torch again.

IV.

Then seem'd the Bard to cope with Time,
    And triumph o'er his doom—
Another world in freshness burst
    Oblivion's mighty tomb !—
Again the hardy Britons rushed
    Like lions to the fight;
While horse and foot—helm, shield, and lance
    Swept by his vision'd sight !

V.

But battle shout and waving plume,
    The drum's heart-stirring beat,
The glittering pomp of prosperous war—
    The rush of million feet—
The magic of the minstrel's song,
    Which told of victories o'er,—
Are sights and sounds the dying king
    Shall see—shall hear no more !

VI.

It was the hour of deep midnight,
　　In the dim and quiet sky,
When, with sable cloak and broider'd pall,
　　A funeral train swept by :
Dull and sad fell the torches' glare
　　On many a stately crest—
They bore the noble warrior-king
　　To his last dark home of rest.

THE BEAUTIFUL.

———

I.

THERE'S beauty in the soft, warm, summer
　　　morn,
When leaves are sparkling with the early dew;
When birds awake, and buds and flowers are born,
And the rich sun appears, half trembling, through
The crimson haze, and dim luxurious blue
Of the far eastern heavens;—there's beauty deep
From mountain-tops to catch the distant view
Of quiet glen—wood-path—wild craggy steep—
Or cool sequester'd coast where lonely waters sleep.

There's beauty in the noontide atmosphere;
When willows bend their graceful boughs to meet
The fountain waters—delicately clear;—
When mid-way heaven the wild lark carols sweet;
There's beauty in the tender traits which fleet
Along the skiey shores and isles of gold,—
That seem just formed for holy angels' feet,—
Gleaming with gifts of an immortal mould !
God, could thy name be lost, while men such scenes
   behold ?

III.

There's beauty in the still, blue hour of night,
When streams sing softly through the moonlit vale;
When, one by one, shoot forth the stars to light,
Dreamy and cold, and spiritually pale:—
There's beauty on the ocean, when the gale
Dashes the merry billows to the strand;
When like a phantom flits some wand'ring sail,
White as the moonbeam on the glittering sand,
And distant flute-notes rise, touched by some skilful
   hand.

IV.

There's beauty on the quiet lake afar,
When wild-birds sleep upon its voiceless breast;—
The lonely mirror of a single star,
Pale shining in the solitary west;

There's harmony and beauty in that rest—
So placid—stirless—lonely—and so deep—
We scarcely move, or dare to whisper—lest
A word should break the magic of that sleep,
And start the spirit nymphs who watch around it keep.

V.

There's beauty on the mountains—when the snow
Of thousand ages on their forehead lies;
Purple and glittering in the sun-set glow,
The gala light of the Italian skies:—
When gorgeously the clear prismatic dyes
Illumine ice-built arches—crystal walls
That, like the Mirrors of the Spheres, arise;
Or proud magician's visionary halls,
Arrayed for merry masques—for pomps and carnivals.

VI.

There's beauty in the old monastic pile,
When purple twilight, like a nun, appears
Bending o'er ruin'd arch—and wasted aisle—
Majestic glories of departed years,—
Whilst dark above the victor-ivy rears
Its sacrilegious banner o'er the shrine,
Once holy with a dying martyr's tears;
Yet amidst dust—and darkness—and decline,
A beauty mantles still the edifice divine!

VII.

All beauty is the Mind's!—The dews of earth,
Her loveliest breathings—her serenest skies
Ne'er warm'd such noble feelings into birth,
As from our own imaginations rise;
The bright, illuminated memories
Which are the rays of the soul's world !—the gay,
And fond creations of our youthful eyes :—
Beauties which set not with the setting day;
But hold a life within—a charm against decay !

THOUGHTS ON THE STARS.

STARS of the solemn night,
    Mute prophets of old time,
What mark ye on your calm and beauteous flight
    O'er distant shore and clime?

Retains the queenly Earth
    Her majesty of air—
The brightness of the morning of her birth,
    When Deity moved there?

Still, silent gaze ye down,
    Pale watchers of the hour;
Miss ye the lost, the old seraphic crown
    God placed in Eden's bower?

Miss ye the seraph-wings
    That dwelt with earth of old?
Shows Night no more the soul-inspiring things
    Her hosts could erst unfold?

Hear ye, by Chebar's stream,
    The angels sing no more?
Fled is the inspiration of that theme?
    Is all its music o'er?

The olive and the vine
    Flourish in beauty still;
But when will shape, or sound, or sight divine,
    Hallow fount, vale, or hill?

Hush'd is the Delphian lute,
    The Olympic laurel gone;
The triumphs of Athenian song are mute;
    But ye, ye still shine on.

I mark ye flashing free,
    Yet marvel 'midst your light
That ye, who watch'd the Saviour's agony,
    Could e'er again look bright.

Empires have shrunk to dust;
    Crowns crumbled 'neath your sway;
Sceptres and thrones, whereon the Mighty trust,
    Fallen, like meaner prey.

Sage, seer, and prophet fam'd,
　　To you their hours have given;
Ye by the bard immortal have been nam'd
　　The poetry of heaven.

And yet not so; if power,
　　Passion, and grandeur, be
The elements of that mysterious dower,
　　Clouds are heaven's poetry:

When they at sunset wear
　　The mantle of their god,
And with their gorgeous presence all the air
　　Seems as by angels trod.

Or when from storm beneath
　　The lightning leaps afar,
Like God's avenging sword from out its sheath—
　　Oh, match not with the star.

The poetry of clouds !
　　The passion and the might,
Which at one stride the howling ocean shrouds.
　　And shakes the throne of Night.

Clouds are heaven's poetry—
　　Whirlwind and tempest make
These their wild heralds o'er the shrieking sea.
　　Whilst hearts with terror ache.

No; beautiful ye are,
    And fair as woman's love;
And to the poet dear is every star
    His eyes yet found above.

But not to you is given
    The character to change,
And mark the varying poetry of heaven—
    Ye have a bounded range.

Nor need the bard deny
    What every moment tells,
Clouds are the mighty *features* of the sky,
    And there expression dwells.

Youth, hope, and beauty, meet
    To celebrate your worth;
Ye to the lover and the muse are sweet
    As aught beheld from earth.

Ye cheer the cloister'd flower,
    When night sits cold and dim;
Or list the lonely nun at twilight-hour
    Breathe low her vesper-hymn.

All sacred feelings seem
    To hail the light ye shed;
Prophets have knelt, and bless'd the starry beam
    That first to Jesus led.

Oh, when my setting day
    Leaves dark the path I trod,
Still lead my thoughts upon your heavenly way,
    And light my soul to God.

'TIS A LOVE-THOUGHT.

'TIS a love-thought hidden
    In a maiden's breast,
    Which, though sweetly chidden.
      Will not let her rest.
She, in golden vision
    Of her love, hath wreath'd
Feelings more Elysian
    Than e'er tongue hath breath'd.

Every sorrow losing
    In the passion wrought,
There she sitteth musing
    O'er her one sweet thought.
Still her fate unseeing,
    Love doth all impart ;
Beauty fills her being,
    Melody her heart.

'TWAS YESTERDAY.

'TWAS yesterday!—oh! solemn sound,
    Heard oft as idle breath,
  Yet, prophet-like, to all around
    It speaks of woe and death!
A mourner by the Past it stands,
    In mystic mantle of decay,—
Shrouds in the night of years its hands,
    And grasps all life away!

High from the boundless vault of time,
    The stars of empire veer:
'Twas yesterday they beam'd sublime,
    The mightiest in their sphere;
'Twas yesterday reveal'd to fate,
    The rival crowns of centuries flown,
Show'd where a phantom sat in state,
    Upon the Cæsar's throne.

We hope,—but what we hope the shroud
    Wraps from our weeping sight;
We aim at stars and clasp the cloud,—
    Seek day, and find but night!

Ah ! who with life's dread woes could cope,
 If 'twere not for that Faith sublime,
Which sees the Ararat of Hope
 Above the floods of time !

What, then, is yesterday ?—a key
 To wisdom most divine,—
It is the hall of memory,
 Where Fame's brief trophies shine :
The spiritual home of things,
 Where intellect immortal beams.
Which lends to thought its holiest wings,—
 Inspires the noblest themes !

A *drop,* that mirrors forth a *world,*
 Then mingles with the earth :
A star from Time's vast empire hurl'd,
 Slow falling from its birth :
A presence with the sacred past,
 To warn our spirits of delay,—
Which saith, "Proud man, to-day *thou hast,*
 Use well thy little day !"

THE SULIOTE.

I.

I LIVE for Immortality,
   And Time to me is nought;
Death hath no torture for the free.
   No power with terror fraught!
Beyond the fetter and the brand,
   The tyrant's red control;
I seek the everlasting land!—
   The Sabbath of the Soul!

II.

Ye urge me to betray the friends,
   For whose brave blood ye thirst;
Show me the bribe your tyrant sends
   To purchase deed so curst!
Display the wealthy argosy,
   This treachery to win;
To blast the counsels of the free—
   And steep my name in sin!

III.

Away! the gold was never found
  That yet might shake my faith:
Bring—bring your felon racks around—
  A Suliote fears not death!—
His home is like the eagle's nest,
  Inviolate and high;
Freedom the idol of his breast,
  For which 'tis *dear* to *die!*

IV.

List!—*'tis* the war-cry of the brave!
  Hear ye that thrilling cheer?—
They come—whose every step's a grave,
  For each assembled here!
Marshall your stern and countless hordes!
  Oh, vain and powerless show!
There lives a spirit in *our* swords
  That *slavery* ne'er may know!

V.

Off!—I have heard a voice that fills
  With treble strength these veins;
Back,—back!—the fire that lights our hills
  Shall melt the tyrant's chains!
God of the Just! be *thou* my shield!
  My fate be in thy hand!—
He dashed amidst the hostile field,—
  He gained his native land!

FAITH.

FROM the anguish of the spirit
        Came a moan,—
A moan of utter dreariness,
A sigh of inward weariness,
        Of confidence o'erthrown !
"When—when shall man have rest?" it cried;
And through the dark on every side,
A voice, half heard, half lost, replied,
        In syllables sublime—
"When thy Faith hath wings to waft her,—
        Light to climb,
Rest shall meet thy soul hereafter !—
        Wait thy time !"

From the giant head of Alps,
Bearded by the avalanche,
Thousands winters yet shall blanch,
        Came a moan;
And the torrents leapt aside,
As above them still replied,
        High in solitude sublime,
" Rest is in the Great hereafter !
        Wait thy time !"

From the broad Atlantic ocean,
With an everlasting motion,
     As in pain,
Swept that wandering voice, distrest,—
"When—oh! when—shall Man have rest?"
And above the raging blast,
That, 'mid clouds, the billows cast,
     Rose a strain,
Higher than the storm could climb,—
" Rest is for the Great Hereafter,
     Wait thy time !"

Then the darkness stept aside,
And the glory multiplied,
   As an avenue of light
   Shewed an angel to the sight:
Slowly to the spirit, chained
Unto sorrow, that complained,-
   She approached—and as she trod,
   Comfort, like a breath of God,
   Fell upon that spirit bent,
   In its own abandonment;
And those eyes, with sudden grace,
Turned upon that angel-face
   With a perfect hope, and said,
   " Blessed be the Holy One !
   Blessed,—may *His* will be done."

And before the words were gone,
Suddenly the angel fled;—
But within that heart renewed,
    Like a chime,
Rang the melody sublime,—
"When thy Faith hath wings to waft her, —
    Light to climb,
Rest shall meet thy soul HEREAFTER!—
    Wait thy time."

A. Ireland and Co., Printers, Manchester.

www.ingramcontent.com/pod-product-compliance
Lightning Source LLC
Chambersburg PA
CBHW022343020726
47500CB00004B/1258